NOTE TO PARENTS

Learning to read is an important skill for all children. It is a big milestone that you can help your child reach. The Richard Scarry Easy Reader program is designed to support you and your child through this process. Developed by reading specialists, each book in the series includes carefully selected words and sentence structures to help children advance from beginner to intermediate to proficient readers.

Here are some tips to keep in mind as you read these books with your child:

First, preview the book together. Read the title. Then look at the cover. Ask your child, "What is happening on the cover? What do you think this book is about?"

Next, skim through the pages of the book and look at the illustrations. This will help your child use the illustrations to understand the story.

Then encourage your child to read. If he or she stumbles over words, try some of these strategies:

- **Use the pictures as clues**
- **Point out words that are repeated**
- **Sound out difficult words**
- **Break up bigger words into smaller chunks**
- **Use the context to lend meaning**

Finally, find out if your child understands what he or she is reading. After you have finished reading, ask, "What happened in this book?"

Above all, understand that each child learns to read at a different rate. Make sure to praise your young reader and provide encouragement along the way!

LEVEL 1

Introduce Your Child to Reading
Simple words and simple sentences encourage beginning readers to sound out words.

LEVEL 2

Your Child Starts to Read
Slightly more difficult words in simple sentences help new readers build confidence.

LEVEL 3

Your Child Reads with Help
More complex words and sentences and longer text lengths help young readers reach reading proficiency.

RICHARD SCARRY'S
Great Big Schoolhouse
Readers

The Mixed-Up Mail Mystery

Illustrated by Huck Scarry
Written by Erica Farber

STERLING

New York / London
www.sterlingpublishing.com/kids

Huckle and Bridget went
to the library.

Huckle loved trains.

Bridget loved mysteries.

When they went outside,
Skip didn't see Huckle.

Huckle didn't see Skip.

"Stop!" called Arthur.

Too late!

CRASH! The bike fell.

The boys fell.

Huckle's book went up in the air.
Something fell out.

It was a letter!

The letter was addressed to:

Miss Mouse
Cheese Street
Busytown

"Why is this old letter in my
train book?" asked Huckle.
"It's a mystery!" said Bridget.

They all went to Cheese Street.

They looked on one side
of the street.

They looked on the other side.

They did not find
Miss Mouse.

They did find Ella and Molly.
"We are looking for Miss Mouse,"
said Huckle.

Arthur bumped into Molly's bike.

The bike rolled away.

"Oops!" said Arthur.

Officer Flossy held up her
stop sign.
"Watch out, Lowly!" said Huckle.

Officer Flossy knew Miss Mouse.

She told them where to find her.

Miss Mouse was in her garden.

Huckle gave her the letter.

Miss Mouse read it:

Dear Miss Mouse,

Do you want
to get some
ice cream?

From,
Toot

"Toot Mouse works in the
train yard," said Arthur.

That gave them a great idea.

They all went to the train yard.

There was Toot!

Miss Mouse smiled at Toot.

Toot smiled at Miss Mouse.

"It has been a long time.
Do you still want to get some
ice cream?" asked Toot.

They all went to get ice cream.

"I love ice cream," said Arthur.

"I love trains," said Huckle.

"I love mysteries," said Bridget.

"I love you," said Miss Mouse.

And that was the happy end
of the mixed-up mail mystery.

STERLING and the distinctive Sterling logo are registered trademarks of Sterling Publishing Co., Inc.

Library of Congress Cataloging-in-Publication Data Available

Lot #: 10 9 8 7 6 5 4 3 2 1
03/11
Published by Sterling Publishing Co., Inc.
387 Park Avenue South, New York, NY 10016

In association with JB Publishing, Inc.
121 West 27th Street, Suite 902, New York, NY 10001

Text © 2011 JB Publishing, Inc.
Illustrations © 2011 Richard Scarry Corporation
All characters are the property of the Richard Scarry Corporation.

Distributed in Canada by Sterling Publishing
c/o Canadian Manda Group, 165 Dufferin Street
Toronto, Ontario, Canada M6K 3H6
Distributed in the United Kingdom by GMC Distribution Services
Castle Place, 166 High Street, Lewes, East Sussex, England BN7 1XU
Distributed in Australia by Capricorn Link (Australia) Pty. Ltd.
P.O. Box 704, Windsor, NSW 2756, Australia

produced by ●JR Sansevere

Sterling ISBN: 978-1-4027-8450-7 (hardcover)
            978-1-4027-7321-1 (paperback)

For information about custom editions, special sales, premium and corporate purchases, please contact Sterling Special Sales Department at 800-805-5489 or specialsales@sterlingpublishing.com.

RICHARD SCARRY'S
Great Big Schoolhouse
Readers

One of the best-selling children's author/illustrators of all time, Richard Scarry has taught generations of children about the world around them—from the alphabet to counting, identifying colors, and even exploring a day at school.

Though Scarry's books are educational, they are beloved for their charming characters, wacky sense of humor, and frenetic energy. Scarry considered himself an entertainer first, and an educator second. He once said, "Everything has an educational value if you look for it. But it's the FUN I want to get across."

A prolific artist, Richard Scarry created more than 300 books, and they have sold over 200 million copies worldwide and have been translated into 30 languages. Richard Scarry died in 1994, but his incredible legacy continues with new books illustrated by his son, Huck Scarry.